This Little Tiger book
belongs to:

_____

_____

_____

For my dad
– S S

For Lily, Holly, Harry, Jack,
Daisy and Ben
– C P

LITTLE TIGER PRESS LTD,
an imprint of the Little Tiger Group
1 Coda Studios, 189 Munster Road, London SW6 6AW
Imported into the EEA by Penguin Random House Ireland,
Morrison Chambers, 32 Nassau Street, Dublin D02 YH68
www.littletiger.co.uk

First published in Great Britain 2022

Printed in China • LTP/2800/4079/0821
10 9 8 7 6 5 4 3 2 1

FSC
www.fsc.org
MIX
Paper from
responsible sources
FSC® C017606

The Forest Stewardship Council® (FSC®) is an international,
non-governmental organisation dedicated to promoting responsible
management of the world's forests. FSC® operates a system of forest
certification and product labelling that allows consumers to identify
wood and wood-based products from well-managed forests.

For more information about the FSC®, please visit their website at www.fsc.org

OCTOPANTS
THE MISSING PIRATE PANTS

Suzy Senior

Claire Powell

LITTLE TIGER
LONDON

Hello, come in and welcome
to our world beneath the sea!

Meet Pufferfish, and Turtle too,
and Octopants – that's me!

I once tried finding pants my shape
and didn't have much luck.
But someone called me "Octopants"
and, well, the name just stuck!

But Pufferfish wears underpants –
he's always got some on.
Though just last week, disaster struck:
his pirate pants were GONE!

"Come on," I said to cheer him up.
"Let's go and track them down!"
So off we went, with lots of snacks,
and searched all over town.

We looked in
Lobster's Laundry . . .

Lobster's
Laundry

SPOTLESS

Mermaid's
Hair

and we checked in
Mermaid's Hair . . .

We tried in Mussel's Fitness Club:
the pants were JUST NOT THERE!

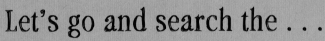

MUSSEL'S FITNESS

"We're out of luck!" sobbed Pufferfish.
"Ohh, what a pointless trek!"
"Hey wait!" I said. "We can't give up.
Let's go and search the . . .

. . . WRECK."

"The shipwreck? YIKES!" yelled Pufferfish.
"It's creepy!" Turtle cried.
"I hope your undies aren't in THERE!"

We bravely peered inside.

But THEN we heard a booming voice:
"Ahoy! Come up, me hearties!
You're just in time to join the fun.
Us pirates LOVE our parties!"

And there they were, a pirate crew
in pants all shapes and sizes:
Pants with anchors, pants with bows,
and pants for cool disguises!

Rainbow pants
and disco pants . . .

and pants to make
you tougher.

Yes, PIRATE PANTS were EVERYWHERE —
but STILL no pants for Puffer!

"You've lost your pants?" the pirates cried.
"I wonder where they arrr?
Don't worry, lad, they'll soon turn up.
They can't have gone too far."

Just then, a shadow crossed the deck.
It all went cold and dark.
We saw a flash of giant teeth
and Turtle shouted . . .

. . ."SHARK!"

"She's after us!" yelled Pufferfish.
"We've got to get away!"

We dodged past ropes and cannon balls,
but then the shark called, "HEY! . . .

I'd like to join your pirate crew.
I've got a hat!" she said.

Then Pufferfish began to laugh,
"My PANTS . . .

. . . are on your HEAD!"

"Your pants?" the shark looked quite surprised.
"I found them in the kelp!
Here have them back."
And Puffer smiled,
"Hey, thanks for all your help!"

"Hooray for pirate pants!" we cheered.
"Let's celebrate!" And SO . . .

We joined the pirates back on board
to PARTY! YO, HO, HO!

More tentacle-tickling rhyming tales from Little Tiger!

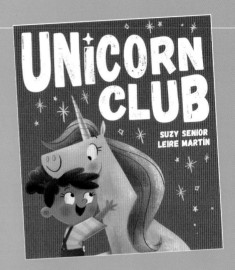

UNICORN CLUB
SUZY SENIOR
LEIRE MARTÍN

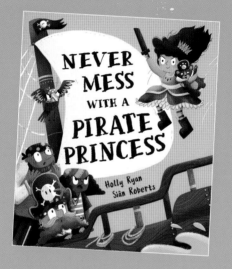

NEVER MESS WITH A PIRATE PRINCESS
Holly Ryan
Siân Roberts

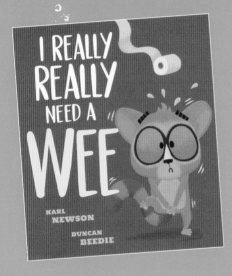

I REALLY REALLY NEED A WEE
KARL NEWSON
DUNCAN BEEDIE

DOCTORSAURUS
EMI-LOU MAY · LEIRE MARTÍN

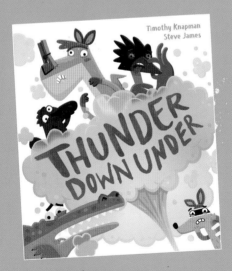

Timothy Knapman
Steve James
THUNDER DOWN UNDER

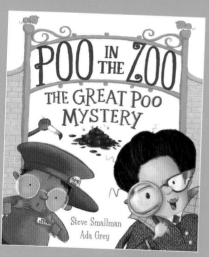

POO IN THE ZOO THE GREAT POO MYSTERY
Steve Smallman
Ada Grey

LITTLE TIGER

For information regarding any of the above titles or for our catalogue, please contact us:
Little Tiger Press Ltd, 1 Coda Studios, 189 Munster Road, London SW6 6AW
Tel: 020 7385 6333 · E-mail: contact@littletiger.co.uk · www.littletiger.co.uk